PRESENTED BY

Lauren Christina Cherry
Second Grade

WESTMINSTER SCHOOLS

SMYTHE GAMBRELL LIBRARY

I Have Heard of a Land

by **JOYCE CAROL THOMAS**

illustrated by **FLOYD COOPER**

JOANNA COTLER BOOKS

An Imprint of HarperCollinsPublishers

For Katrina Joy Pecot
—J C T

For Mama
—F C

I Have Heard of a Land
Text copyright © 1998 by Joyce Carol Thomas
Illustrations copyright © 1998 by Floyd Cooper
Printed in the U.S.A. All rights reserved.
http://www.harperchildrens.com

Library of Congress Cataloging-in-Publication Data
Thomas, Joyce Carol.
   I have heard of a land / by Joyce Carol Thomas ; illustrated by
Floyd Cooper.
       p.   cm.
   "Joanna Cotler Books."
   Summary: Describes the joys and hardships experienced by an
African-American pioneer woman who staked a claim for free land in
the Oklahoma Territory.
   ISBN 0-06-023477-6. — ISBN 0-06-023478-4 (lib. bdg.)
   1. Oklahoma—History—Land Rush, 1889—Juvenile Fiction.
[1. Oklahoma—History—Land Rush, 1889—Fiction.   2. Frontier and
pioneer life—Fiction.   3. Afro-Americans—Fiction.]   I. Cooper,
Floyd, ill.   II. Title.
PZ7.T36696Iae   1998   95-48791
[E]—dc20   CIP
                                                                        AC

Designed by Christine Kettner
3   4   5   6   7   8   9   10
❖

I have heard of a land
Where the earth is red with promises
Where the redbud trees catch the light
And throw it in a game of sunbeams and shadow
Back and forth to the cottonwood trees

I have heard of a land

Where a pioneer only has to lift up her feet

To cast her eyes on the rocks

The fertile earth, the laughing creek

Lift up her feet running for the land

As though running for her life

And in the running claim it

The stake is life and the work that goes into it

I have heard of a land
Where the cottonwood trees are innocent
Where the coyote's call is a lullaby at night
And the land runs on forever
And a woman can plant her crop and
    walk all day and never come to the end of it

I have heard of a land
Where the imagination has no fences
Where what is dreamed one night
Is accomplished the next day

I have heard of a land where the flapjacks
Spread out big as wagon wheels
Where the butter is the color of melted sun
And the syrup is honey
Stirred thick by a thousand honeybees

I have heard of a land
Where winter brings storm warnings
And pioneers wonder whether
The scissortail in spring will ever sing

I have heard of a land where the children
Swing in homemade swings strung from
The strong limbs of trees

I have heard of a land
Where the crickets skirl in harmony
And babies wrapped to their mothers' backs in the field
  laugh more than they cry

I have heard of a land where worship
Takes place in an outdoor church
Under an arbor of bushes
And the hymns sound just as sweet

I have heard of a land
Where a woman sleeps in a sod hut
   dug deep in the heart of the earth
Her roof is decorated with brush
A hole in the ground is her stove
And a horse saddle is her pillow
She wakes thinking of a three-room log cabin

And soon that morning her neighbors
   and their sons and daughters
Help lift the logs and chock them into place
Together they hoist the beams high
After dinner, they finish the porch
   where they sit and tell stories
Finally when everyone else has gone home
She saws the planks for the steps
   by herself

That night by the glow of an oil lamp
She writes in her journal:

> I raise nearly everything I eat
> The land is good here
> I grind corn for meal
> Raise me some cane and make sorghum syrup
> And if I feel real smart
> I make hominy grits from scratch

I have heard of a land
Where the pioneer woman still lives
Her possibilities reach as far
As her eyes can see
And as far as our imaginations
    can carry us

AUTHOR'S NOTE

I Have Heard of a Land was inspired by my family's westward journey to Oklahoma. I wondered how they unearthed the courage to strike out for parts unknown, to turn their dreams into action. What encouraged them, and other Blacks, to leave everything they knew behind and travel west?

Many Blacks in the South were drawn to the posters about the 1889 and 1893 land runs, in which they could stake a claim for free land. At the shot of a gun, the posters announced, a runner (or a rider or a wagon driver) could race as far as he or she could go and claim that stretch of land as his or her own. The word was that the Oklahoma Territory was a place where industrious Blacks could build a life free from fear. Many were attracted by the promises of titles to lots, free railroad tickets, and by Black newspapers— created by the new Black communities springing up—that sang the praises of liberty in a land called Oklahoma.

In addition, the Oklahoma Territory was one of the few places where a single woman could own land in her own name. The lone woman in *I Have Heard of a Land* recalls one of those women. In Ponca City, Oklahoma, where I was born and raised, there stands a statue of the Pioneer Woman, holding her young child's hand.

My mother's side of the family was among the group who ran the land on foot. In 1893, my great-grandparents, Charlie and Judy Graham, set out for Oklahoma on a wagon train with about 300 other families from Tennessee. My great-grandma Judy liked to tell her granddaughter, my aunt Corine, of the time their wagon came to a raging river. They had to cross the river, but there was no bridge. As they started across, the water began to rise until everyone trembled with fear. When the horses got frightened, Great-Grandpa climbed out of the wagon, stepped between the horses, grabbed their bridles, and began to lead them across the turbulent river. Just before he reached dry land, the current got so swift that it began to carry Great-Grandpa and the horses away. Great-Grandma stood up in the wagon, raised her hands toward heaven, and started to pray a fervent prayer. Evidently her powerful prayer was heard, because the horses stopped thrashing and walked the family safely on across the river.

My aunt Corine remembered the story of their journey and the run. And it is my aunt Corine who has passed along to me the story of how my pioneer great-grandma slept in a dugout and grew "row feed," which she ground into cornmeal that fed my pioneer family so long ago.

The settling of African-Americans in Oklahoma is a complex story of flight from the South, where ex-slaves still suffered the insults brought about by the horrors of slavery. It is a story of Black settlers surviving and thriving. And for a moment in history, it is the story of cooperation among Blacks, Whites, and Native Americans in the West.

I Have Heard of a Land is one story of the journey of African-Americans to a place of hope, a hope connected to the yearning for land—when land was another word for freedom.

—Joyce Carol Thomas